A Gift for Giving

Yasmine Case

Copyright © 2022 Yasmine Case

All rights reserved.

ISBN: 9798806304378

This Book Belongs To:

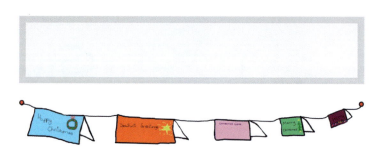

"I'm so excited" sang Theodore, as he danced around the living room. Theodore and his mum were busy decorating the Christmas tree in preparation for Christmas Day. "It looks beautiful" smiled Mum.

A Gift for Giving

After decorating the tree, Theodore sat quietly and began to write a letter. He was very excited for Christmas this year. On his letter to Santa, he is asking for a Mega Robot Rocket 2000. Theodore knew that he had to be good all year. He has been very helpful around the house, tidying, helping with the washing up and lots of other jobs.

A Gift for Giving

Once Theodore had finished his letter to Santa, his mum helped write the address and put a stamp on it.

They got ready to go to the post box to post his special letter.

He wrapped up warm with his hat and gloves, he even put his favourite red wellies on.

A Gift for Giving

After a little walk they found the post box. Theodore's Mum lifted him up so he could post his letter.

As they walked home Theodore's Mum commented "When we get home, you need to put some toys away, you have so many. You are very lucky; some children don't have anything."

Theodore thought about what his mum said for the rest of the way home.

When they arrived home Theodore went straight to his bedroom and put his toys away. As he was doing this, he thought about all the children who don't have very much, and how he could help.

Suddenly, Theodore had a fabulous idea. "I can buy gifts for giving."

Theodore ran over to his money box and emptied the money onto the floor, but sadly there wasn't enough money inside it. He sat feeling sad, when he suddenly remembered what his mum had told him.

She said, "You have so many toys, you are very lucky."

From this Theodore had the most amazing idea.

"I will give the children my toys, they would make the best gifts for the children that don't have very much."

Theodore went and told his mum about his plan. When she heard that he wanted to give his toys to other children, she was very proud and said, "What a fantastic idea."

A Gift for Giving

Theodore did not have much time to prepare his gifts for giving, so he spent the next few days finding, cleaning and wrapping the toys. It would be a lot of work, but Theodore knew with a little help from his mum he could get the job done.

After all his hard work, he had finally finished wrapping all the gifts. He had one more job to do and that was to write the Christmas cards.

In each card he wrote "This gift I am giving is yours, to make you smile on Christmas Day. Your friend Theodore."

A Gift for Giving

Theodore put the gifts in a bag and then put the bag onto his sledge so he could pull the gifts through the snow.

One door at a time, Theodore placed a gift at a child's door. Once he put the gift down, he knocked on the door and then hid. He wanted each gift to be magical for every child.

There was only one gift left. He placed it next to the door and was about to hide when the door began to open. Stood before Theodore was a sad little girl he recognized from school. It was his friend Ellie.

They smiled at each other; she was happy as she saw her friend. Theodore picked up the gift and passed it to Ellie. A big smile spread across her face, and she got a twinkle in her eye.

"WOW", she shouted "This is the best Christmas gift ever, thank you so much." This made Theodore very happy, and they gave each other a big hug.

Early the next day Theodore rubbed his eyes as he got out of bed, when he suddenly realised it was Christmas Day. He ran into the living room and saw the gifts under the tree. There were gifts from mum and a gift from Santa.

A Gift for Giving

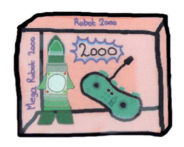

Theodore had one last gift to open, he shook it to guess what was inside. He took his time unwrapping his final gift. As the last piece of paper was peeled back, he couldn't help but shout "It's a Mega Robot Rocket 2000, I can't believe it!". It was hard to hide just how happy he was with his present.

A Gift for Giving

While playing with his toys on Christmas Day, Theodore thought of his friends and children he had given to. While he was playing, his mum came in and told him he had received a letter. They read the letter together. It was a thank you letter from Ellie. Theodore commented "WOW, I really did make a difference."

A Gift for Giving

From then on, every year Theodore sorted his toys and picked the best ones to give. He named it the Christmas gift for giving tradition.

ABOUT THE AUTHOR

Yasmine Case is an Early Years Educator by day and a new children's story book author by night. She has a real passion for writing and illustrating children's stories and receives a great deal of inspiration from working with her audience. Yasmine writes sweet, fun, inspiring and educational books for young children.

Printed in Poland
by Amazon Fulfillment
Poland Sp. z o.o., Wrocław